Gugu's House

Gugu's House

Catherine Stock

Clarion Books  New York

For Mrs. Khosa and for my mother, two fine artists

Clarion Books • a Houghton Mifflin Company imprint • 215 Park Avenue South • New York, NY 10003 • The illustrations were executed in watercolor. • The text was set in 16-point Esprit Book. • www.houghtonmifflinbooks.com • Printed in Singapore • Library of Congress Cataloging-in-Publication Data • Stock, Catherine. • Gugu's house / by Catherine Stock. • p. cm. • Summary: Kukamba loves helping her grandmother decorate her mud home in a dusty Zimbabwe village, but when the annual rains partially destroy all her work, Kukamba learns to see the goodness of the rains. • ISBN 0-618-00389-4 • [1. Grandmothers—Fiction. 2. Zimbabwe—Fiction. 3. Artists—Fiction. 4. Rain and rainfall—Fiction.] I. Title. • PZ7.S8635 Gu 2001 [E]—dc21 00-043009 • TWP 10 9 8 7 6 5 4 3 2 1

"Come, my little one," called Gugu. "We will have a cool drink of water as soon as we get home."

"I'm coming, Gugu." Kukamba struggled to keep up with her grandmother as they walked along the long, dusty path from the bus stop. The sun beat down and her bundle was heavy. She couldn't wait to get to Gugu's house.

Kukamba loved visiting Gugu. No one in the city had a beautiful rambling house like hers. There were wild elephants sculpted and painted on the compound walls. There was an airplane flying over the courtyard gate. Best of all was the big painted zebra Kukamba mounted to gallop across the dry grassy veldt.

Every morning after breakfast, the men in the village set off with their livestock to find fresh grazing and the women set off to tend their crops. Kukamba stayed in the village to help Gugu.

They fed the chickens.

They swept the house and courtyard clean with long brushes.

They fetched water from the well.

They collected firewood.

Then Gugu and Kukamba worked on the house. Gugu mixed mud and dung to make new walls and animals. She showed Kukamba how to shape little zebras, leopards, birds, and lions.

While the sun baked the walls dry and hard, Gugu collected ash from last night's fire for white paint, and charcoal to crush into black paint. Kukamba scooped clay from the riverbed to mix into red paint. In the kraal they found cattle dung to pound into green paint. They squatted in the shady side of the courtyard to grind the colors with stones.

MAFUMAKADZI VHUSIWA
VHURA NDI MBEVHA
MAVHALA NDIZWIL
ZWAMATO
8773212

Gugu gave Kukamba a brush she had made from goat hairs. Kukamba carefully mixed water into the colored powders and began to paint. Sometimes her lines wobbled a little bit, but Gugu didn't seem to notice. "*Heh*. That is a beautiful zebra, my child. You are going to be a very fine artist one day."

Kukamba trembled with excitement. An artist! Like Gugu? "Can I come and paint with you next year too, Gugu?"

"Next year and the year after that and the year after that too." Gugu clucked her tongue and smiled her big toothy smile.

In the evening, the women arrived home from the fields. Tired and hot, they sighed because the rains were late and *aish!* there wasn't enough water for the maize and vegetables.

The feverish day faded into a feverish night and the men came home. Hot and tired, they grumbled because the bore holes were drying up and turning salty and *aish!* there wasn't enough grazing for the cattle and goats. No one noticed Kukamba's paintings.

After supper, everyone sat around the fire in a circle, weary and irritable.

Kukamba climbed into Gugu's lap. "Tell us a Rabbit story, please, Gugu," she whispered.

Gugu's head was as full of stories as her house was full of animals. She poked the fire with a long stick, looking for a good one.

"Tell the one about the race with the tortoise." It was Kukamba's favorite.

Eh, heh! Gugu's eyes twinkled. Even though she had told the story of the race between the rabbit and the tortoise many times, it would surely raise everyone's spirits.

The villagers listened expectantly, waiting for the end:

At last that old Rabbit finished the race. Aish! But there was that Tortoise again, waiting for him, just like at the baobab tree and at the river and at the koppie!

That Rabbit—he just sat down and cried and cried.

"Cheer up, Rabbit," said Tortoise.

"Cheer up, Rabbit," said Tortoise.

"Cheer up, Rabbit," said Tortoise.

"Cheer up, Rabbit," said Tortoise.

Rabbit looked up. Aikona! There were four *tortoises clucking sympathetically around him!*

Rabbit just stared at all those tortoises.

Then he slapped the ground. "Yo-weh! You devils tricked me."

Everyone laughed and laughed. For days afterward when people passed Gugu's house, they remembered her story. "Cheer up, Rabbit," they'd call out to each other, and chuckle.

Finally, one night while the people slept, a thick blanket of clouds crept slowly over the sky and blotted out the small bright stars and the thin crescent moon.

Bvuma . . . Thunder rumbled slowly across the sky and echoed over the veldt. *Bvuma . . . bvuma . . .*

One by one, the people came out of their huts rubbing the sleep from their eyes. A few drops of rain spluttered and sizzled on the warm stones around the fireplace.

Suddenly, a flash of lightning ripped open the clouds and heavy curtains of rain tumbled down to the parched earth.

"U-lu-lu-lu-lu-luu!" trilled the women in their singing voices. Gugu clapped her hands and hugged Kukamba. The men grabbed their wives and danced around crazily. *Yoh-yoh-yoh!* Even the dogs chased each other in circles, barking like mad things.

It rained heavily for several days.

At last, Kukamba awoke to a bright sunny morning.

Aish! All Gugu's paintings had washed away, and some of the courtyard walls were falling down! The great zebra was just a soggy mound of mud.

"*Yo-weh,* Gugu!" cried Kukamba. "Look what that terrible storm has done to your house!"

Gugu was already sweeping the water out of the courtyard with her brush. "The storm was not terrible, my precious," she said. "The storm brought us rain, which blesses the land so plants can grow and the animals have food to eat."

"But, Gugu, what has happened to all our beautiful colors? There is only brown mud everywhere," wailed Kukamba.

Gugu smiled. “Come, my little one, and I will show you where all the colors have gone.” She took Kukamba’s hand and together they walked out into the hills over a carpet of yellow duiweltjies.

A plum-colored starling whistled from the branches of a flowering baobab, and masked weavers wove nests among the fluffy lavender and yellow lantern flowers in the sicklebush.

Gugu waved her hand up to the trees like a magician and then rested it lightly on Kukamba’s small shoulder. “There are your colors, little one,” Gugu said softly. “See how the rain has washed them clean and hung them out to dry.”

Kukamba gazed around her. Then she remembered the muddy house and she tugged her grandmother's hand. "Come, Gugu," she said. "We have work to do."

"Heh!" Gugu clapped her hands. "The house is waiting for us. Let's go!"

Author's Note

The character of Gugu is based on Mrs. Khosa, who lives in a desolate, dry part of Zimbabwe near the Limpopo River. The soil is poor and life is a struggle for the people there, especially during periods of drought. But Mrs. Khosa's colorful house is always full of neighbors, especially children. The stories she tells are found in various forms all over Africa; many of them crossed the Atlantic in the days of slavery and became known here as the Brer Rabbit stories.

Shortly after the rains arrive, water from the Botswana catchment rumbles down the dry Limpopo riverbed, unearthing large terrapins, frogs, and catfish that have been lying dormant in the caked mud. Then fresh green leaves shoot out of the ground and buds burst out of the twiggy brown bush in a riot of color. Almost immediately birds and animals appear, as though they too had been lying dormant in the dust, waiting for the rain.

Vanessa Bristow

After the rains every year, Mrs. Khosa, a deeply religious woman, begins rebuilding her house. The last time I visited her, I was welcomed by a great eland instead of the great zebra. Coming home through the fresh green countryside one summer evening after a thunderstorm, I suddenly felt and understood Mrs. Khosa's optimism and joy. These words and pictures are my tribute to Mrs. Khosa and her very special spirit.

Glossary

Afrikaans (af-ri-KANS): a South African language derived from Dutch

Aikona! (hi-CAW-na): an exclamation of surprise, a bit like "Wow!" or "Gee!"

aish! (HI-eeshhhhh): an emphatic expression

baobab (BAY-oh-bab): a fat-trunked tree with heavily folded bark

bore hole: a well

bvuma (pronounced the way it is spelled): Venda word for thunder

duiweltjies (DOY-vel-kees): pretty yellow flowers that hide a sharp thorn; Afrikaans for little devils

Gugu (GOO-goo): Venda word for grandmother

koppie (KOP-ee): Afrikaans word for little hill

kraal (KRAHL): an animal enclosure

Kukamba (koo-KAM-ba): a Venda name meaning little tortoise

Limpopo River (lim-POE-poe): a large river that flows only during the rainy season; it forms the border between South Africa and Zimbabwe

maize: corn used to make porridge, a staple in the sub-Saharan diet

U-lu-lu-lu-lu-luu!: a high-pitched call women make in times of great emotion, broken by the tongue moving up and down

veldt (VELT): a flat grassy plain

Venda: a language of northern South Africa and southern Zimbabwe

Yo-weh! (GHYOH-way): an exclamation of astonishment and disbelief made with a lot of windy sound, like "Whew!"

Zimbabwe (zim-BOB-way): a country in southern Africa